TITIKSHA

TITIKSHA

A MESSAGE FOR MY FUTURE DAUGHTER

ISHITA MISHRA

PAPER TOWNS
PUBLISHERS

PAPER TOWNS
PUBLISHERS

First published by

Papertowns Publishers

72, Vishwanath Dham Colony,

Niwaru Road, Jhotwara,

Jaipur, 302012

Titiksha

ISBN Print Book – 978-93-6185-776-8

Printed in India

"आज नहीं आज अपने हाथ से खा लो" की तुम्हारी ज़िद्द और "खिलाना तो पड़ेगा" पर मेरा अड़ना।
कभी तुम्हारी रोटी तो कभी तुम्हारी गोदी के लिए सबसे लड़ना।
अब याद आता बहुत आता है।
मेरे दर्द में तुम्हारा दर्द, मेरा एक्जाम जैसे तुम्हारा युद्ध।
उफ़, अब किस्से करू शिकायते सबकी?
किसको गिनती दू की रुलाया किस किस ने?
अब तो देख ऊपर आकाश में, आखों में आसूं भर कह लेती हू उससे "बस कुछ समय और"।
समय की गिनती न याद है ना करना चाहती हूं,
चोट पड़े जब दुनिया से, तकिया को तुम्हारा पल्लू समझ छुप जाती हूं।
नानी, आज मेरी खुद की पहली किताब छपने जा रही है।
जब आऊंगी तुम्हारे पास, तब आकर पूछूंगी, "कैसा लगा?"
मुझे पता है, आज तुम होती तो सबसे ज़्यादा खुश होती।
तुम आज भी मेरी सब कुछ हो, और हमेशा रहोगी।
"ये किताब तुमसे मिले प्यार का प्रतिबिंब है।

ACKNOWLEDGEMENT

This book is a tribute to the journey of love, strength, and the unspoken bonds that shape us. To my mother, the first architect of this dream, who once imagined a name Titiksha for my future daughter. Though not always expressive, she poured her love into the smallest acts: waking up before us, offering dahi-shakkar before every exam, and standing silently as the strongest pillar in my life. She made me strong, emotionally intelligent, and resilient in ways unknown even to her.

To my father, whose quiet presence has always been my shield and whose words few but powerful remind me that I am capable of anything.

To my dog, the child I mothered before my own, who taught me unconditional love, patience, and the simple joy of being someone's safe place.

To myself, the daughter who once longed for wings and now chooses to be them. I had to be my own parent to navigate emotions I wish I had been guided through. And in doing so, I have promised myself my daughter will never have to do it alone. She will never fear being misunderstood, never hold back her dreams, and never shrink to fit into the mold of "*acche bacche aisa nahi karte.*"

And finally, to you, dear reader. Raise daughters who will rule the world, not just obey it. Raise them to carve their own kingdoms, not just fit into societal norms. Give them love, give them freedom, and most of all, give them *you*.

With love,
Ishita Mishra.

To the daughters who mothered themselves,
who sought love in echoes and warmth in absence.

Go, carve your kingdom not to fit, not to please,
but because you were never meant to be caged.

Let them call you wild, let them call you defiant
They have no name for the fire that won't burn out.

PROLOGUE

There was a time when I longed for words that were never spoken, for warmth I had to seek within myself. I learned strength from silence, resilience from absence, and love from the spaces between what was given and what was needed.

This book is my bridge between generations the daughter I once was and the mother I will become. It is a promise to my future, woven with the lessons I have carried and the love I will give freely. *Titiksha* endurance, patience, grace in the storm this name was chosen long before she was even a thought, whispered by my mother, the woman who shaped me in ways she never realized.

I write these words so that when my daughter stumbles, she will find my hands already there to steady her. When she questions herself, she will hear my voice reminding her of her worth. When the world tells her to shrink, she will remember that she was born to take up space, to carve her own kingdom not to crave the world's approval.

This is for the daughters who had to mother themselves, for the ones who searched for their father's love in other men, for those who needed more than just love they needed to be fought for. This is for the daughters who became warriors.

To you, my little one when the world calls you rebellious, smile. It is the world that owes you, not the other way around.

CONTENTS

To The Ones Who Made Me

Dear Mumma & Papa,

Thank you for being the best parents anyone could ask for. You have given me everything in your capacity love, strength, and the freedom to be myself. Mumma, thank you for giving me the idea of this name, a name that now holds so much meaning. Papa, thank you for giving me wings and for making me believe that I could write this book and that it could be a blockbuster.

I know I may have complained at times, but no complaint will ever be big enough to make your love feel small in my heart. You have always tried to move along with time, to be our friends, and to understand us. That effort means the world to me.

I am who I am because of you. And for that, I will always be grateful.

With love,
Your Daughter

Unsaid, Yet Understood

In every step I've taken, in every dream I've chased,
Your love has been the constant, in every challenge I've faced.
Your hands have held me, your words have guided me,
Through every storm, through every gentle breeze.

Mom, your embrace was my first world,
Dad, your strength my unwavering shield.
In your eyes, I found the courage to soar,
In your hearts, I always knew I was adored.

When life felt heavy, you lightened the load,
With every sacrifice, you built my road.
Your love has been the spark in every fight,
The quiet strength that made my world bright.

With you, I learned to never give up,
To rise after falling, to never stop.
Your dreams became my wings to fly,
Your belief in me taught me to touch the sky.

Through every laughter, every tear,
I've felt your love, always near.
Your sacrifices, too many to count,
But your love, immeasurable, knows no amount.

I stand where I am today, because of you,
In every victory, I see your love through and through.
Mom, Dad, you are the reason I strive,
With you by my side, I feel alive.

To the One I've Yet to hold

Dear Titiksha (TiTi),

Your name was meant to be mine, but one random day in 2025, your Nani decided that it would belong to you. And just like that, you became a part of my dreams long before you arrived. I don't know if I'm there with you as you read this, but I want you to know that every word in this book is my way of being by your side. No matter where life takes us, one thing is certain I will choose a wonderful father for you. Someone who will love you in a way no one else can, who will protect you, and who will teach you the kind of strength that runs in your blood.

This book is for you to hold your hand through the tough times, the ones I struggled with. I will make you a fighter, my love, but I will also be the shield you hold when the battles feel too heavy. I hope these words bring you comfort, courage, and a reminder that you are never alone.

With all my love,
Ishita.

Before I Knew You, I Loved You

With every word I write today,
I see you in a distant way.
A name, a thought, a gentle spark,
A tiny soul within my heart.

Titiksha, you are not yet here,
But in my mind, you feel so near.
Curly hair and rosy lips,
A smile that softens my fingertips.

I see your hands, so small, so new,
You will be papa's world, his dream come true.
The way you'll laugh, the way you'll shine,
A love so deep, forever mine.

Through you, my childhood will rewind,
My parents' joy, their hearts entwined.
A mirror of me, yet bold, so free,
A fire, a fighter, meant to be.

And though today, I write alone,
With ink and dreams, your name is sewn.
A daughter, a hope, my love so true
Titiksha, one day, I'll hold on to you.

My Universe in Tiny Fingers

A heart so full, it barely stands.
Pain lingers, but I don't care,
Because, my love, you are there.

Like Rachel held Emma, eyes full of awe,
I cradle you close, no single flaw.
But unlike her, I had a name,
Titiksha, my strength, my heart aflame.

Tiny fingers, a sleepy face,
Your little eyes fight to find their place.
The world can wait, this moment's mine,
To hold you close, to stop all time.

Even as Papa waits in awe,
Even as Nani reaches her palm,
"Let me hold her," they softly plead,
But not yet not from me.

I hear my mother's words so clear,
"You'll understand when she is near."
I used to laugh, I used to roam,
I guess I understand now, Mumma I'm home.

One day, my love, I'll let you go,
But not today just hold me slow.

The First Of Many, But Never Alone

In no time, my love, you will grow,
From tiny fingers to steps so slow.
You'll crawl, you'll stand, you'll learn to speak,
Your laughter, the melody my heart will seek.

You'll bite your toys when your gums feel sore,
Fall sick, and I'll cry even more.
On vaccination days, I'll hold you tight,
Wiping your tears, hiding my fright.

But, my love, your first battle will be mine,
The day I leave for work in time.
My heart will ache, my soul will bend,
Yet my love for you will never end.

Titiksha, a name so fierce, so true
It holds the strength I see in you.
It means to endure, to rise, to stay,
To face the storms, to find your way.

I promise, my child, through night and day,
You'll never feel I'm far away.
You'll never be alone, not once, not ever,
Mumma will love you, always and forever.

I will go to work, but not to part,
To show you strength, to give you heart.
For you, my love, must one day see,
Your mother is a fighter and so will you be.

A Word that will Redefine me

A tiny voice, so soft, so sweet,
A sound that made my heart skip a beat.
"Maa," you called, and time stood still,
A moment no one could ever steal.

Tears filled my eyes, joy filled my soul,
This little word my heart made whole.
I ran to tell the world outside,
With love so big, so deep, so wide.

Your father waits, he tries, he pleads,
"Say Dadda!" but you don't concede.
Yet every "Maa" brings a smile so bright,
Two little teeth, pure joy, pure light.

Titiksha your name, your grace,
Strength and patience in your embrace.
You are my courage, my heart, my fight,
My love, my soul, my guiding light.

And if the world should ever test,
Know, my love, you'll always rest,
In arms that cherish, arms so free,
For my whole world begins with thee.

Daddy's Little Rebel

I never shared the bond I longed for,
A friendship with my father, nothing more.
But, my love, for you, I swear,
I'll choose a father beyond compare.

A man who lifts you when you fall,
Who makes you feel ten feet tall.
Who holds your hand through fear and fight,
Who tucks you in and hugs you tight.

I want you to run to him first,
For every joy, for every hurt.
For the mildest sneeze, the smallest pain,
For silly jokes in pouring rain.

May he be your gym buddy strong,
May he teach you sports all along.
May he cheer the loudest in the stands,
May he hold your dreams in steady hands.

Like the moon and stars above,
I want you to shine in his love.
No need for Mumma to stand between,
For every wish, for every dream.

And, my love, because he'll be true,
You'll never seek his love in someone new.
You won't search in strangers' eyes,
For what was yours pure, no disguise.

For Titiksha means to stand so tall,
To bear, to rise, to face it all.
And with your father by your side,
You'll walk with strength, with love, with pride.

Tiny Steps, Giant Leap

Today, my love, you wore your blues,
Tiny shoes, with untied loops.
Your bag too big, your hands so small,
Yet you stood so brave, so tall.

My heart swelled with pride and care,
Watching you step out, unaware
That this journey, just begun today,
Will shape your dreams in every way.

I won't impose, I won't demand,
Just walk ahead, I'll hold your hand.
Come home, my love, tell me it all,
Every laugh, each rise, each fall.

Some days Mumma might be caught in race,
But I promise, love, I'll never erase,
The stories you bring, the joys you share,
I'll listen, I'll cherish, I'll always be there.

We'll do homework side by side,
Paint the animals, let colors collide.
Draw on walls? Call your friends?
Mumma's love will never end.

If alphabets wobble or numbers run wild,
If nineteen's tricky, don't fear, my child.
We will learn, we will try, we will fall, we will rise,
Together, forever, through all of life's highs.

So go, my star, explore and shine,
Your journey is yours, but your heart is mine.
And no matter what this world may do,
Mumma will always, always love you.

No Roads Lead You Away from Home

One day, my love, my little star,
You will shine in a world that's ours.
I will build a life, strong and true,
And choose a father who'll adore you too.

Work will call, and dreams will rise,
Yet your laughter will light up our skies.
Some days will be busy, some nights will be long,
But in your heart, love will stay strong.

You will never tiptoe, afraid of my voice,
I will not shout you'll always have choice.
No slammed doors, no angry cries,
No fear hidden behind your eyes.

I will not let my burdens fall,
Upon your tiny hands so small.
You will not bear the weight I carry,
Your heart will never feel heavy or wary.

If tears must fall, they will wait,
Until you sleep, safe and late.
You'll never feel like you're the cause,
Of weary sighs or hurried pause.

We work, my love, not just for you,
But for our dreams, for what is due.
You are not a debt, not a load,
You are the brightest light on our road.

And if storms arise, as sometimes they do,
You'll never stand in the shadow's view.
No anger will reach you, no careless fight,
Will steal away your peaceful night.

No raised voices will shake your ground,
No cruel words will ever sound.
If you falter, if you fall,
My arms will always break your fall.

We will build a home where love is free,
A space for you to simply be.
No matter how busy, no matter how blue,
Our hearts will always come back to you.

And when the world outside is cold,
Our walls will be of warmth untold.
You will laugh, you will shine,
With love so deep, forever mine.

A Win Etched in Gold

My little star, my shining light,
You are strong, you are bright.
Not just to win or race ahead,
But to stand tall, no matter what's said.

Some days, kids may laugh and tease,
Say words that hurt, and steal your peace.
Some days, you may not be picked to play,
And it might make you sad that day.

But listen, love, and hear me say,
Your worth won't ever fade away.
Your name Titiksha means to stay,
To stand up strong, to find your way.

Your first victory won't need a prize,
Not claps, not trophies, not cheering cries.
Your first victory would be a step to participate,
To try again, not fear the weight.

It will come when you take a chance,
Even if you miss a dance.
It will come when you wipe your tears,
And push away your little fears.

Maybe you'll stumble, maybe you'll fall,
Maybe you won't remember it all.
Maybe your hands will shake today,
But you'll still stand and find your way.

And when you come to me at night,
With stories of how you chose to fight,
Even if it's just a tiny start,
Know that you have won my heart.

Because my love, my precious one,
Winning isn't always fun.
It's in the trying, it's in the fall,
It's in getting up and standing tall.

So don't give up, don't hide away,
I'll be right here, every day.
With open arms and love so true,
To remind you there's nothing you can't do.

The Pain that Crowned You A Woman

Slow down, my love, don't grow up so soon,
I still see you dancing under the silver moon.
Tiny hands that once fit in mine,
Now reaching for dreams that shine divine.

One day, my baby, your time will arrive,
A change will come, and you'll feel so alive.
But I'll be here, right by your side,
With open arms, my heart open wide.

When I was little, I didn't quite know,
How strong we are, how much we grow.
But you, my love, will never fear,
For I'll be here, always near.

That pain will come, but so will care,
A warm hug, soft hands running through your hair.
Hot water bags, a bed so tight,
Your favorite snacks and movies all night.

Cry if you must, or rest in my arms,
There's no shame, no fear, no alarms.
I will not hush your sighs and moans,
Your pain is real you are never alone.

And not just me, my love, you'll see,
Your father too will bring you tea.
He'll warm your bags, he'll pat your back,
For love like ours will never lack.

I'll teach you strength, to stand up tall,
To buy your pads, to fear no call.
For being a girl is not a sin,
It's where life itself begins.

Not just the first, but every time,
You'll have my love like a nursery rhyme.
Because, my queen, you deserve it all,
On period days, and days so small.

I know you're growing, I see it clear,
But stay my baby, just one more year.
I'll hold you close, I won't let go,
Even as you bloom, just so you know.

For in my arms, you'll always stay,
My little girl, forever that way.

A Roar in Ribbons

They'll stare at you, my child,
Not with kindness, but with eyes that crawl,
Tracing lines they have no right to see
As if your worth lies skin-deep, not soul-high.

Some might follow you home,
Even when you're just a girl with books and dreams,
And worse some may wear faces you trust,
A relative, a neighbor... the world hides monsters well.

But hear me now, my Titiksha
You were not born to bow, to hush, or to hide.
You hold the sharpest weapon in your tiny frame
Your Voice.
Let it blaze.

Scream.
Shout.
Yell his shame to the winds,
Let the silence shatter like glass at your feet.
The world may call it defiance
But I'll call it survival, I'll call it strength.

You will not wait for a man to shield you,
You will not seek permission to feel safe.
You are not a flower to be plucked or pitied
You are a lioness with ribbons in your hair
And fury in your bones.

And should your voice ever tremble,
Know that mine is behind yours
Ten thousand thunderbolts of a mother's wrath.
No judge, no uncle, no passerby,
Will hear your pain and walk away unburnt.

My daughter,
You were not made to endure in silence
You were born to roar,
To tear shame apart at the seams,
To guard your dignity like sacred ground.

So let them try
Let them test your strength,
Let them forget who your mother is.

They will learn.
The world will learn
That my daughter does not break.
She breaks them.

A Mother's Promise

And if ever your voice shakes,
Mine will roar for you,
Until yours finds its way again.

You are never alone, Titiksha.
Mumma is your shield, your echo, your safe place.

First Crush, First Butterflies

One day, my love, the world will change,
A new kind of feeling exciting, yet strange.
Your heart will race, your cheeks may flush,
You'll tell me, "Mumma, I think it's a crush."

And I'll smile, my darling, and hold you near,
For love and wonder, there's nothing to fear.
It's normal, it's sweet, it's just how we grow,
A fleeting breeze, a gentle glow.

Your dad and I, we'll always be here,
To hear your whispers, to calm your fear.
No hiding, no shame, no silent sighs,
Just stories of smiles and twinkling eyes.

But listen, my love, as I take your hand,
There's so much to learn, so much to understand.
Not every glance, not every touch,
Means something deep it's not always much.

Holding hands? It's okay, my dear,
But know when to pause, know when to steer.
Your heart may be curious, your body too,
But patience, my love, will carry you through.

For love is magic, but it takes time,
It's more than a spark, it's more than a rhyme.
One day, you'll know when the moment is right,
But for now, just dance in the soft moonlight.

Feel the butterflies, let them be,
Enjoy the stories, share them with me.
For no matter what, through every new phase,
I'll be your safe place, always, always

The Ache Of First Love

One day, my love, your heart may ache,
A boy you liked might not feel the same.
He may smile at you, then turn away,
Or whisper sweet things, yet not stay.

You might wonder, Was I not enough?
Pick apart your smile, your laugh, your touch.
You'll stare at the mirror, searching your face,
Trying to find what you'd want to replace.

But my girl, my love, lift your chin,
You are magic, the universe within.
No boy, no glance, no fleeting crush,
Can ever define your worth so much.

It's okay to cry, to feel the sting,
To replay moments, overthinking everything.
And when you do, I'll sit by your side,
We'll roll our eyes, mock his silly pride.

Your dad, oh love, will pace the floor,
Muttering threats of settling the score.
But you and I, we'll laugh instead,
Eat ice cream, watch movies, and rest your head.

Because heartbreaks fade, and so will this,
One day, you'll look back and almost miss
The way you loved so purc, so truc,
And realized that love starts with you.

So walk ahead, head held high,
No man defines your fire inside.
You, my girl, are your father's pride,
A queen who needs no one to shine.

And when the right love finds its way,
You'll know it's real, you'll choose to stay.
But until then, dance, be wild and free,
Because no heartbreak will ever take you from me

Chasing Success, Choosing Yourself

The day will come, my love, my light,
When books pile high and dreams take flight.
Exams will whisper, "Do your best,"
And you might feel life's little test.

But listen, my girl, hear me say,
Your worth is not a grade today.
Numbers, scores they come and go,
But what you are is what you know.

You are laughter, bold and bright,
A curious mind, a fearless sight.
You are hands that build, a heart that feels,
A soul that dreams, a strength that heals.

You have the wisdom of those before,
Your nani, her mother scholars galore!
And your mumma, oh, she stands tall,
Not for scores, but through it all.

So we will read, we will learn,
We will try and take our turn.
But if the numbers seem unfair,
We'll smile and breathe we'll get there.

Because my love, you are a queen,
With fire, with courage, with grace unseen.
We work hard, not to prove we're good,
But because we can we should.

And through the ups and through the lows,
Through every test that life bestows,
I'll stand beside you, strong and true,
My baby girl, I believe in you.

A Scar That Shapes, Not Breaks

One day, my love, you may sit and cry,
For friends who left without a goodbye.
The ones you trusted with all your heart,
Might walk away, might drift apart.

Secrets spilled, laughter turned cold,
Stories untold, hands left to fold.
The ones you thought would stand so true,
Might choose another path, leaving you.

And my love, I know it will ache,
A silent storm, a heart that breaks.
You'll wonder why, you'll question how,
You'll wish to fix it, here and now.

But listen close, my precious one,
Friendships fade, but life goes on.
For every bond that comes undone,
Another will form, just like the sun.

At every stage, through every year,
New hands will hold, new hearts draw near.
Some may stay and some may leave,
But you, my love, will never grieve.

Because through it all, through loss and gain,
Through sunny smiles and days of rain,
One thing is sure, one thing is true,
Your dad and I we choose you.

No secrets held, no tales untold,
No love withdrawn, no hand left cold.
We won't tell you to turn away,
We'll listen first, we'll let you say.

We'll share our lessons, we'll let you choose,
For you, my love, will never lose.
You'll rise above, you'll learn to see,
That true love stays just like me.

And if the world should bring you low,
If darkness whispers, dims your glow,
Remember this you are enough,
You are Titiksha, fierce and tough.

No betrayal, no wound, no fall,
Can break you, my love, you have it all.

So, let them go, let them fade,
Your light, my love, will never jade.
Because in this life, one thing is true,
You will always have me and you

The Silence That Roars

One day, my love, you might feel alone,
A weight in your heart, a silence unknown.
You'll search for a friend, a hand to hold,
A place where your stories can safely unfold.

You might think, "They won't understand,"
That your parents are far, like castles on sand.
You'll crave the voices of friends instead,
Needing laughter to clear your head.

There will be moments you close your door,
Not wanting our voices anymore.
You'll roll your eyes, you'll sigh, you'll fight,
Thinking we don't know what feels right.

And I? I will let you be,
I'll watch you grow, I'll set you free.
I won't ask you to stay inside,
Or tell you to push your thoughts aside.

I will never say, "Acche bacche aisa nahi karte,"
For you, my love, are more than a role to play.
You are Titiksha strong and free,
A girl who will bloom in her own way.

If one day, your world feels too small,
If loneliness builds like an endless wall,
Know that my arms are always wide,
No matter how far, I'm by your side.

If friends forget, if they turn away,
If words unsaid lead hearts astray,
You may not want me to always stay,
But I will wait, just a breath away.

No burden too heavy, no story too small,
No distance too great, just give me a call.
I'll listen, I'll laugh, I'll cry with you,
For my love, that's what mothers do.

You may walk ahead, as far as you please,
But love, we'll always be the softest breeze.
So when the nights feel a little too long,
When your heart hums a lonely song,
Remember, my love, no matter how far,
You are my Titiksha, my brightest star

The War Within You

My dearest Titiksha,

There will be days when shadows creep in,
When you question your place in this world.
When the mirror seems unkind,
And your heart feels weighed down by doubt.

You will see others racing ahead,
Reaching milestones you have yet to touch.
You might feel lost, left behind,
But my love, your journey is yours alone.

I will never let silence be my answer,
Never let you sit alone in sorrow.
I will never say, "Acche bacche aisa nahi karte,"
Because my darling, you are already enough.

No whisper of the world can change your worth,
No stumble can take away your light.
If your heart is heavy, if you feel like you've failed,
Look at me, my love I will always believe in you.

You are Titiksha resilient and strong,
A soul meant to rise, no matter how long it takes.
The sky does not rush the stars to shine,
And you, too, will glow in your time.

Your father and I will walk beside you,
Not to push, not to scold,
But to lift you up when you feel small,
To whisper, "Try again, my love."

If you ever feel unworthy,
If you think you've let us down,
Remember this, my precious one
You could never disappoint the ones who love you.

Let no grade, no comparison, no harsh word,
Make you believe you are anything less than extraordinary.
You are our pride, our light, our love,
And no matter what, we will always have your back.

So stand tall, my strong, beautiful girl,
For you are capable of conquering the world.
The world is waiting for your light to shine,
And I promise you you will win it all, in your own time.

Crossroads

One day, you'll sit with questions too heavy,
Dreams pulling you in different ways.
The world will ask, "What will you become?"
And you may not have an answer to say.

The roads ahead may twist and turn,
Some paved, some wild, some unknown.
You may fear taking a step too soon,
Or worry you'll have to walk alone.

But my love, you are never alone,
Nor bound to a single lane.
Your life is not a script to follow,
But a story only you can frame.

I will never hand you my broken dreams,
Or weigh you down with what I missed.
You are not born to fulfill my wishes,
But to create your own list.

Try, explore, take a step and see,
If one path closes, another will be.
You do not fail by changing your mind,
You fail only if you refuse to try.

No "accha baccha" burden, no guilt to bear,
No dream too small, no choice unfair.
You are Titiksha strong, unshaken,
Through storms of doubt, you will awaken.

And if you ever feel lost, my love,
If the weight of the world is too much to hold,
Look beside you, feel our hands,
Your father and I will walk with you, bold.

So dream, my girl, and dream aloud,
Fear not the whispers of the crowd.
For the sky does not rush the stars to shine,
And your time, my love, will always be divine

Find the One Who Feels Like Home

One day, love will knock on your door,
Not a fleeting crush, not a passing breeze,
But a love that feels like home,
Like the warmth of sunlight through the trees.

This time, it won't be just butterflies,
Not just stolen glances, whispered names,
This time, it will be steady, strong,
A love that stays, not just a game.

And my love, when that day arrives,
Know that your heart is safe with us.
We will not doubt, we will not judge,
For we trust the love you trust.

But my darling, remember this too
A love worth keeping is one that stays true.
A love that stands, just like your father,
One who lifts you, not one who bothers.

Find a man who listens with care,
Who stands by you when life's unfair.
One whose love is not just words,
But actions louder than what's heard.

A man who sees your fire and light,
Who never dims, but makes it bright.
One who holds you in laughter and pain,
And never makes you love in vain.

This time, you will not stand alone,
No shame, no fear, no need to hide.
For your father and I will stand beside you,
With hearts open, arms stretched wide.

So love, my girl, love without fear,
Let it be deep, let it be true.
And when you find a love like your father's,
knowthat it will have my blessing, too.

You are Titiksha strong, unafraid,
And love will find you when it's time.
And when it does, my darling girl,
May it be a love as rare as mine

You Are More Than a Moment

My dearest child, my heart, my light,
Through every storm, through every night,
You'll never walk this path alone,
For in our love, you have a home.

The world may whisper, judge, and frown,
Make you feel lost, make you feel down,
But hear me now, and hold this tight
You are not wrong, just not on time.

If love has touched you, soft and deep,
If passion woke you from your sleep,
Do not let guilt weigh down your soul,
Your heart is pure, your spirit whole.

If wine should call you once or twice,
To taste, to laugh, to break the ice,
You need not hide, you need not lie,
We'll pour the glass and stand nearby.

If distant lands should call your name,
Adventure's spark, the traveler's flame,
Go, my love, and see, and roam
With our blessing, with our love, come home.

You'll never need to stand alone,
Or script your words in practiced tone,
For we are more than just your guide,
We are your home, your place to confide.

A house of peace, a love so true,
A heart that always beats for you,
With every choice, with every fall,
We stand beside you through it all.

So live, my child, be wild, be free,
And know you're always safe with me.

Your Light Never Dims

I gave you a name with hope so wide,
A name that would keep your spark alive.
But long before you came to me,
You lived within my destiny.

I know the weight of unheard cries,
Of silent wars behind my eyes.
Of being there, yet left behind,
Of love that came, but never in time.

But you, my child, will never wait,
For love, for care, for twists of fate.
If you whisper, I will hear,
If you stumble, I'll be near.

No pleading eyes, no silent pain,
No waiting long, no love in vain.
If you need me, I will stay,
No distance, no excuse, no delay.

No forced visits, no words unsaid,
No thoughts locked up inside your head.
Your urgency will be my own,
Your heart will never beat alone.

I once faded in the background's haze,
Left unseen in love's cruel maze.
But you, my child, will never know,
The ache of being second-row.

For as I breathe and as I stand,
You are the first to hold my hand.
You are the light, the spark, the flame,
And I will never dim your name.

The Fire Within

My love, my rebel, my wildflower,
There will be days when a fire stirs within,
When your body whispers secrets of longing,
And you wonder if wanting is a sin.

The world will tell you to hush,
To bury your desires in guilt and shame,
To deny the heat in your veins,
As if pleasure is a woman's blame.

But hear me, my love, my daughter,
You are not wicked, you are not wrong.
Your body is a song of nature,
And every note belongs.

There is no shame in hunger,
No guilt in what you crave.
To know yourself is power,
To understand is to be brave.

Come to me with your questions,
Let's speak without fear.
No walls, no locked doors,
No whispers drowned in tears.

You are not alone in this journey,
I was once where you stand.
I too wondered, I too felt,
I too searched to understand.

So study, explore, and listen,
Learn what it means to be free.
For you are not just a daughter,
You are a woman, like me.

And in this home, my dearest,
You will never walk in shame.
The fire within you is yours to own,
And I will never let them dim its flame.

Crowned by birth

My love, you were not born to yield,
To bow, to break, or to be concealed.
You were made to rise, to shine, to stand,
To build your world with your own hand.

They'll say, "Be quiet, be small, be sweet,"
But you were never made for defeat.
You are the fire, the storm, the sea,
Unchained, untamed forever free.

Your voice will shake the tallest walls,
Your courage echo through the halls.
Men may flinch, the world may stare,
But you, my love, will never scare.

Yet power alone is not your grace,
Love still softens every space.
Be bold, be fierce, but gentle too,
The world needs strength
And warmth from you.

And when they ask,
"Who taught you to be this way?"
Smile, my love,
And tell them
"My mother did."

Untamed, Unapologetically You

Write, my love, till the stars grow dim,
Sing your song, or dance on a whim.
Paint the skies or chase the seas,
Do whatever sets your heart at ease.

If words are your world, then write away,
Till dawn turns into dusk each day.
Not for fame, nor for a prize,
But for the joy that lights your eyes.

No dream's too big, no wish too wild,
You are my heart, my fearless child.
And should the world not understand,
Know, my love, I'll hold your hand.

We'll laugh, we'll cry, we'll scream, we'll shout,
But we'll figure it all, there's no doubt.
If we fight, don't run, don't hide,
Just wait till dinner I'll be on your side.

For I won't love you from afar,
I'll love you right for who you are.
Not how I was, nor what they see,
But how I wished love felt for me.

So when they ask, with envy or pride,
"Who's your hero? Your heart, your guide?"
You'll grin and say, with mischief at hand
"My mother, my chaos, my best friend!"

Between Us, Only Light

Back when I was young, trust came with doubt,
Every call, every text someone snooped around.
Sneaky glances, suspicious stares,
Like my thoughts were public wares.

But you, my love, will never see,
A world where trust is locked with a key.
Your phone can lie open, no need to fear,
For I'll never pry I'm always near.

No snatching, no shouting, no rules unfair,
No "acche bacche don't do this, beware!"
Talk of crushes? Let's chat away,
Your mum was young once what can I say?

When the world says, "Spoiled your girl, you see?"
I'll smile and say, "She's wild and free!"
For rebels aren't made from trust and cheer,
But from silence, guilt, and unspoken fear.

So bring me the gossip, the texts to decode,
We'll craft perfect replies your mum's a pro!
And when love confuses your tender heart,
I'll guide you through, no falling apart.

We'll binge-watch Friends, it's a sacred test,
If Joey's not your fave, I'll be distressed!
But no worries, my love, we'll figure it out,
Through laughter, through hugs, and zero doubt.

For you're not just my daughter you're my pride,
No secrets, no shame, nothing to hide.
Hand in hand, through thick and through thin,
In this mad, mad world together, we win.

Wings, Not Cages

They'll tell you to sit, to smile, to stay,
To walk a line, the "right" old way.
But darling, hear me loud and clear
Their rules don't matter, not in here.

Wear your shorts, ink your skin,
Dance in the rain, let the wild begin.
Let no hand tame the fire in you,
Burn bright, my love, break every view.

They'll say, "A girl should act this way,"
But you'll make your own damn play.
You'll choose your love, your heart's delight,
But trust me, he must pass my sight.

Spend your money, splurge, be free,
Until you learn to invest like me.
Fall, rise, and chase your dreams,
Life's a mess, but it's as grand as it seems.

And when the world may raise its brow,
Your father will stand, protect, and vow.
No man will match the love he shows,
For in his eyes, you wear the rose.

And though I know, it's plain to see,
You'll love your dad more than me.
But that's okay, I'll stand aside,
With knowing smiles, and endless pride.

So, live, my love, as wild as the sea,
You write the rules you set yourself free.

Love is All About Balance

Love, my child, is not a test,
Not a weight upon your chest.
It's not just giving, not just care,
But feeling safe when he is there.

You are not his mother, dear,
Not the one to chase his fear.
You're his partner, strong and free,
Love's not a cage it's meant to be.

Speak your heart, your needs are true,
He must hear and cherish you.
Love's not silence, love's not pain,
It's sunshine bright, not endless rain.

There will be days of peace and light,
When love feels easy, pure, and right.
And days that ask for patient grace,
For hearts to grow, for love's embrace.

So dream together, side by side,
Through storm and sun, through low and high.
But never shrink, don't dim your fire,
Love should lift, should not require

To lose yourself, to fade away,
For love should never make you stray.
Stand your ground and set your pace,
Find love that feels like home, like grace.

Not a Contract, But a Promise

Marriage, my love, is not a trade,
Not a bargain, not a debt repaid.
Not a script with rehearsed lines,
But a dance of hearts, a love that shines.

It isn't about losing, nor being owned,
But standing beside, not kneeling alone.
Not a cage, nor chains to wear,
But a promise of love, tender and fair.

You will not leave, you will not fade,
The girl we raised, the bonds we made.
Your name may change, your home might too,
But, my love, you will always be you.

His home welcomes, his arms embrace,
But your roots will never be replaced.
You are a daughter, a sister, a friend,
A love that time will never bend.

Love his mother as your own,
For she once rocked him, skin to bone.
Honor her love, but never forget,
The home that raised you with no regret.

Two families now, a bridge, not chains,
Love should flow, not bring you pain.
Balance, my child, with steady grace,
Hold your own, but make them a place.

Be his partner, not his shadow,
Walk beside, not behind to follow.
Speak your heart, your dreams, your fire,
Build a love that lifts you higher.

Know his needs, but know your own,
In love, respect must be sown.
Give, but never fade away,
Marriage is love, not self-betrayal's way.

And even as you take his name,
Your father's love will stay the same.
No distance, no time, no vow can sever,
You were his girl, and will be forever.

And when they say, "You are now theirs,"
Stand tall, my love, push past the stares.
For marriage is love, not a cage or bind,
It's two hearts growing, two souls aligned.

So go, my love, love strong, love true,
But never forget, you are still you.

Your Life, Your Call

My love, your life is yours to steer,
To chase the stars or hold home near.
Be a dreamer, be a doer, be still, be wild,
Be whatever sings to your heart, my child.

If you wish to build a world outside,
To hustle, to soar, to stand with pride,
Then run, my love, and claim your place,
Let no voice dim your burning grace.

Let your hands shape dreams into gold,
Stand unshaken, fierce and bold.
Break the glass, rewrite the rules,
For you were never meant for cages or tools.

And if home is where your passion stays,
If love is built in quiet ways,
Then stay, create, and make it bright,
For there is power in warmth and light.

A home is not surrender, nor a lesser call,
It is a kingdom, built with love so tall.
A queen within, a heart so free,
That none shall ever question thee.

You are Titiksha, my fearless one,
Not bound by roles, nor by anyone.
Not by whispers, nor by rules,
For I have raised no one's fool.

No choice is small, no path is wrong,
As long as you remain strong.
So work, create, or rest and be
Whatever you choose, let it set you free.

And when the world leaves you lost and torn,
When questions sting, when dreams feel worn,
Come to me, my love, come home, stand tall
For I named you so, to rise through all.

Your life is yours, my love, my star,
And no decision will take you far,
From the love that raised you, bold and bright,
To walk your path, in peace or fight.

So stand, my love, on hills or sand,
With fire in heart, and love in hand.
For whether you build, or choose to stay,
The world is yours in every way.

Your Room Shall Wait

One day, my love, you'll step away,
With dreams in your eyes, finding your way.
The echoes of laughter, the warmth of your touch,
Will linger in corners that miss you so much.

Your cupboard will stand, just as you left,
No hands will touch, no space bereft.
Not for a guest, nor another to claim,
For it holds your scent, your name, your flame.

The books you stacked, the notes you penned,
The tiny keepsakes, the letters unsent,
All will remain, untouched, unchanged,
A silent promise, a love unstrained.

Your bed will wait, the pillows will know,
The weight of your dreams, the stories they hold.
Not a single frame will be set aside,
For this is your home, your soul's pride.

No younger sibling will take your space,
No guest will rest in your embrace.
Your name is carved in every door,
A love that lingers forevermore.

Go, my child, and chase the skies,
Let the world see the fire in your eyes.
But know this home, these walls, this place,
Will always hold your heart's embrace.

And when the storms feel too unkind,
When the world forgets to remind,
Turn back, my love, come see, come stay,
For this is home it never fades away.

From a Distance, I Will Watch

It is time, my love, for you to rise,
To chase the sun, to claim the skies.
The girl I raised, fierce and free,
Now stands tall for the world to see.

I will watch from a distance, silent, proud,
Cheering for you, though lost in the crowd.
I'll glare at you when you doubt your might,
And smile when you set the world alight.

Your battles are yours, but I'll always be near,
A shadow of love, a whisper you hear.
Through victories bright and struggles deep,
My faith in you, forever will keep.

Go, my love, hustle and win,
Break the barriers, let life begin.
And when you soar, don't look around,
Just know in your heart I'm always proud.

When You Become a Mother

One day, my love, you will cradle life,
A tiny heartbeat resting near yours,
The world will gather, eyes filled with awe,
Adoring the miracle you brought forth.

They will count the fingers, kiss the toes,
Marvel at the softness of newborn skin,
They will call you strong, they will call you brave,
For the love you pour, the warmth within.

But as they celebrate the mother in you,
Your father and I will look beyond,
For in that quiet, tender moment,
We will still see our little one.

The tiny hands that once held ours,
The sleepy eyes that searched for home,
The giggles that filled our silent nights,
The child we raised, now fully grown.

As you whisper lullabies in the dark,
As you rock your baby near your chest,
Know that in every tired sigh,
You are living the love you once possessed.

And when the world calls you Mama,
With pride and joy, your heart unfurls,
We will smile and hold you close,
For before she was yours you were ours.

If I Am Not There

You are a dream I hold so close,
A whisper in time, a promise untold.
Tomorrow, you'll be my living reality,
But what if fate leaves my hands cold?
What if I'm not there to guide your way,
To brush your hair or hold your hand?
What if I can't be the voice you seek,
When life turns tides you don't understand?

But, my love, don't you ever fear,
For even if I am just a trace,
This book will hold my heart for you,
Every word, a warm embrace.
Your father will know, he'll hand this down,
A piece of me, forever near.
A guide to life, my love for you,
So even in absence, I'll still be here.

You are cherished, beyond all time,
Even now, though you're a dream to me.
And if one day we never meet,
Know, my child you were always free.
Free to dream, to love, to fight,
To carve your path, to rise, to be.
You are my forever, my silent wish,
And I will always live in thee.

And when the world feels dark and cold,
And you wonder where your strength is told,
Remember, my love, it lives in you,
In everything you say and do.

👼

In every tear that falls from your eyes,
In every smile that lights the skies,
In every step you bravely take,
Know, my child, it's love you make.

If I'm not there to wipe your tears,
To calm your doubts, to quell your fears,
Know, my love, I'll be a spark,
Guiding you when life gets dark.
Through every storm, through every fight,
I'll be with you, holding you tight.
And in your heart, you'll feel me near,
A whisper, a song, a love so clear.

For though I may not walk beside,
You'll feel my love as your guide.
In every breath, in every prayer,
In every moment, I'll be there.
So go, my child, and spread your wings,
Take life's lessons, embrace what it brings.
And in your heart, you'll always find,
A piece of me, forever kind.

EPILOGUE

Final Reflection & Encouragement

My Dearest Daughter,

As you read these words, know that every thought, every poem, every letter, has been written with the deepest love I could offer. This book is not just a collection of lessons or dreams it is a part of my heart, given to you, to hold onto whenever you need strength, guidance, or comfort.

Life is not always a smooth path. There will be moments when you feel lost, when you question your choices, when the world feels overwhelming. But remember, my love, every challenge you face is an opportunity to grow, to become the woman you were always meant to be. You will stumble, but you will rise. You will face pain, but you will find healing. You will feel doubt, but you will discover your strength. Never forget, you are made of resilience and grace.

You are the culmination of all that I have taught, all that I have hoped, and all that I have wished for you. But now, it's your turn to carry forward this legacy. With every step you take, with every decision you make, you will write your own story, and I will always be with you in the pages.

Embrace life with open arms, with courage and compassion. Remember that you are never alone, even when it feels that way. The love we share transcends time and space, and it will guide you through every chapter of your life, just as it has guided me to this moment.

My dear, be brave. Be kind. Be fierce. Be free.

You are my forever, and I will always be with you, in your heart, in your dreams, and in every word you speak. Go forth, my child, and live the life I always dreamed for you full of strength, love, and endless possibility.

With all the love a mother could give,

From a mother every that daughter needs.

Bonus Page: A Message from the Heart

Titiksha was just a name, a fleeting thought. First, it was meant to be my name, then the name of my daughter, and now, it has become a reality. A book, a collection of poems, letters, and messages meant for her a daughter who is still a dream in my heart, a thought that blossoms in the deepest corners of my soul. And yet, in these thoughts, I have found the mother I am becoming, the mother I always wished I could be.

The journey of motherhood began not with the idea of a child, but with a presence that made me realize what was already stirring in me. My dog, Sultan, brought out in me the tenderness, the care, and the fierce love that I never knew I had. From that moment, I knew in my heart that one day, I would make a great mother. I knew I would choose the best father for my daughter, someone who would be everything she deserves. I would protect her, guide her, and love her with every beat of my heart. And in those dreams, I saw you, meri beti.

Titiksha, once a mere thought, now feels so real to me. My heart swells with love for you, even though you are not yet here. I can't fathom how something so intangible, something so unseen, can feel so alive within me. The love I have for you, the bond I feel for you, is a force beyond understanding. It is as if I already know you, meri jaan the one who will one day call me 'Maa'. How could something so pure, so beautiful, be only a thought? Yet, here I am, pouring all the love I have into these words, into this book.

This book, Titiksha, is not just a collection of poems. It is my heart, my dreams, my deepest desires for you. Each word here is a seed planted with hope, each line a prayer whispered for your future. Every poem is an echo of the love I have felt for you since the moment I first imagined you. Every page is my wish for you to be strong, to be fearless, to be everything you are meant to be.

I have lived many years as a daughter, and in those years, I have gathered the wisdom and lessons I hope to pass down to you. I have become the mother I once longed for a mother who will always stand by you, even in your darkest moments. A mother who will encourage you to chase your dreams, to soar high, and to never give up on your heart's deepest desires. A mother who will guide you through every heartbreak, every struggle, every triumph. A mother who will teach you that love is both fierce and gentle, that it is a force that can heal and empower.

It is hard to imagine that you, my dear, are still just a thought, a khwaab I carry in my soul. And yet, in every heartbeat, I know you are real. You are a part of me, and I am already a part of you. This book, my love, is more than just pages filled with words. It is the essence of my love for you. It is my legacy, my gift to you, a piece of my heart that you will carry with you, forever.

I cannot wait to meet you, to hold you in my arms, to whisper all the things I've dreamed of telling you. But until that moment comes, know that you are cherished, you are loved beyond measure, and you will always have my heart, meri beti.

This is not just a book; it is a bond that will never be broken, a love that will never fade. And one day, when you read these words, I want you to feel my embrace, to feel my love wrap around you like a warm blanket, protecting you from the cold winds of life.

Until we meet, you will always live within me. And when we finally come face to face, know that you are the fulfillment of every dream I've ever had, meri pyaari Titiksha.

AUTHOR'S NOTE

To my dearest daughter,

Writing this book has been one of the most profound and emotional journeys of my life. As I put pen to paper, each word seemed to flow from a place deep within me, a place I never knew existed until I started to imagine you the little girl who is yet just a thought but already so loved. *Titiksha* is not merely a collection of poems, it is a reflection of my dreams, my hopes, my fears, and above all, my love for you, a love that grows stronger every day, even though you are not yet in my arms.

The idea of *Titiksha* began as a name a name I first thought of for myself, then for you, my daughter. And as I pondered what it would mean to raise you, to guide you through life, I realized that this name would become more than just a label. It would become a symbol, a constant reminder of resilience, love, and strength values I want you to carry within you as you grow.

In writing this book, I poured my heart and soul into every poem, every message, and every story. It was not just an act of writing, but an act of living through my emotions, of imagining what it would be like to be the mother I always wished I had, and to give you the love, strength, and wisdom you need to thrive in this world.

This book is a gift to you a gift that transcends time, a piece of me that will always be with you. Every word here is a reflection of the hopes I have for your future, the love I want to share with you, and the bond I want to build between us, even before you are born. It is a promise that, no matter where life takes us, I will always be by your side, guiding you, supporting you, and loving you with every part of my being.

Through *Titiksha*, I hope you will feel the essence of who I am and who I hope you will become. I hope this book gives you strength during difficult times, comfort in moments of doubt, and encouragement to follow your dreams. More than anything, I hope that when you read these words, you will feel the warmth of my love so strong, so boundless, that it will reach across time and space, wrapping you in a mother's embrace, no matter where you are in your life.

My dear, know that you are the greatest blessing of my life, and in you, I see all my hopes and dreams come alive. I cannot wait to meet you, to hold you, and to guide you through the journey of life, just as this book will guide you now.

"तुम मेरी उम्मीदों का आकाश हो, और मैं तुम्हारा पहला सूरज। तुम्हारी हर मुस्कान में मेरी दुनिया बसती है, और तुम्हारी हर आहट में मुझे अपनी धड़कन सुनाई देती है। तुम मेरे दिल का अनकहा प्यार हो, जो शब्दों में नहीं, बल्कि हर पल में महसूस होता है।"

With all my love,
Future Mom.

Titiksha – A Reflection for You:

1. What does the name 'Titiksha' mean to you?

   ___

2. Which poem in this book touched you the most, and why?

   ___

3. In the poem about 'Her First Heartbreak,' what feelings did it stir within you?

   ___

4. What dreams do you hold for the person you love most, whether it's your daughter, a loved one, or yourself?

   ___

5. What advice from this book do you think will help you in times of struggle?

   ___

6. What is the most important lesson you would want to pass on to your child, or to someone you love deeply?

   ___

7. If you could write a letter to your future self, what would it say?

___

8. Reflecting on the concept of motherhood (or fatherhood), how do you envision your relationship with your children?

___

9. How do you deal with challenges in life, and what do you do to stay resilient?

___

10. In what ways have the poems in this book changed your perspective on life, love, and relationships?

___

We'd Love to Hear From You!

Your thoughts and reflections mean the world to us. If you feel inspired, we'd be honored to hear how *Titiksha* touched your heart and any insights you gained from this journey.

Please feel free to share your reviews, personal reflections, or responses to the questions above by emailing us at: [ishita.mishra0101@gmail.com]

Your words are an invaluable part of this experience, and we look forward to hearing from you.

With love,
The Author

ABOUT THE AUTHOR

Ishita Mishra is a passionate poet, writer and a woman with high ambitions. Born and raised in Kanpur, Uttar Pradesh, Ishita's journey has been shaped by her experiences, a love for writing, and the unwavering support of her family. With a background in graduation and post-graduation from Delhi, she has always been a diligent student, participating in anthologies and becoming a published author.

Ishita's writing finds its roots in her deep emotional connections, particularly with her nani, who was her greatest support and inspiration. Losing her in 2017 was a defining moment in her life, and *Titiksha* is a heartfelt tribute to the love and wisdom she received from her.

Her journey toward writing *Titiksha* began with a conversation with her mother, where the name "Titiksha" was originally meant for her but was later passed on to her future daughter. This sparked a flood of emotions and led her to create this book a collection of poems and messages meant to inspire daughters and mothers alike.

Through *Titiksha*, Ishita wishes to convey a message to all daughters that they are enough just as they are, not bound by societal expectations, and should follow the path guided by their hearts. She also encourages parents to love their daughters so deeply that they never feel the need to seek love elsewhere.

Ishita's ultimate mission with this book is to offer daughters, especially those struggling to find love at home, a source of warmth, affection, and support. Her journey is a testament to the belief that one can overcome any obstacle with love, strength, and resilience.